PERSPECTIVE

LENS

PERSPECTIVE LENS

by

Mary Duffy

DIADEM BOOKS

PERSPECTIVE LENS

Copyright © 2019 **Mary Duffy**
This edition 2023

Published by Diadem Books

ISBN: 9798867120894

Foreword

Title: *Perspective lens*

Before you read, I wish to explain that there is more than one way to understand this book with its involved storylines. This, of course, depends entirely on the reader.

Chapter One

EVA was fourteen years old and a thin girl of average height and build. She had blue eyes and brown wavy untamed long hair which was usually tied up at the back with an elastic band. Eva's clothing was not of the latest fashion and she was not a stranger to wearing hand-me-down garments from people in the neighbourhood or relatives. Although Eva wasn't used to having things go her way early on in life it never stopped her—she wasn't one for dwelling on happenings. Eva's understanding of life was there is a reason for every season, and she carried on with a positive mind-set whatever the weather.

Today, however, was different. Eva struggled to see her way through the darkness of what was coming that Thursday afternoon. At some point in time the family dog Bess had escaped through the back gate which resulted in her having pups. There had been several efforts to find a home for the pups as Pete, Eva's guardian, could not afford another addition to the costly outgoings he was struggling to manage. While they were looking to house the pups, Eva had become quite attached to them, giving them names, and one in particular would follow her around the house, jumping on her laces whenever she would pass the pup by.

Pete was raising Eva alone after her parents passed away Eva couldn't remember them as she was only four years old when they passed on. Pete was Eva's uncle on her father's side and the closest relative to Eva, so he took Eva into his home to care for her. Pete was a tall man with short black hair and would usually be seen in his work overalls and with dirty hands from working in the warehouse. Eva thought there was a lot of lifting of boxes as he would often complain about his backache. He worked two jobs to keep a roof over their heads and he was often stressed because of financial pressure.

One afternoon, Pete had become so despondent with his state of affairs that he sat with his head in his hand for some time. It was obvious he was coming to what appeared to be the end of his tether. Eva thought he was having some kind of breakdown. As she watched him closely, she was startled when he suddenly jerked quickly with a glazed look on his face, placing the bills on the side of the table. Then in a moment of madness, Pete rose from his seat and grabbed a sack from the nearby cupboard and, one by one, took the three pups and placed them inside the sack before heading for the back door with the sack over his shoulder. Eva could hear the pups yelping as Pete left the house. As he did so Eva followed after him.

'What you doing, Pete?' asked Eva. Pete's pace was fast and Eva lagged behind just trying to keep up. 'Pete, I can take the pups to my friend's,' she continued, saying anything she could to stop him as she dreaded the worst. Pete carried on, still with that glazed gaze in his eyes, through the fields, until he arrived at River Stone bank. It was raining and the river was high and flowed fast, and Eva was afraid of what was going to happen next.

'*Please*, Pete, don't do it, let me take them home!' She was pleading by this time, trying to change his mind. Covered in mud from the riverbank, Eva fell to her knees before quickly scrambling back to her feet in a hurry to catch him up. Pete grabbed her.

'Shut up, Eva! Shut your mouth!' He threatened Eva to be silent, fearful that someone had noticed what was about to happen. Whilst the sound of the pups barking came from the bag, Eva was desperately hoping that someone would hear.

'Please, Pete, I'll do anything, don't do it!' she pleaded.

Like hot water boiling, Eva could feel her anger rising, bubbling up with nowhere to go. Then a paralysing state of shock and desperation consumed her, and she couldn't think straight. Eva was usually one to have a plan or a way around most situations but not this time; this time she felt powerless with an overpowering feeling of hopelessness.

She could feel its darkness consuming her, recognising two extremes of each other, a polarity, the feeling of powerlessness and power recognising each other, two totally different states yet connected extremes.

Too late, it was all over. Eva stood sobbing as the river carried the sack down far away from where they stood. Pete took Eva's arm, dragging her through the undergrowth heading back towards home. When they arrived home, Eva could hardly breathe, looking at him carefully and afraid, trying not to let him catch her staring at him. Her eyes smouldered in silence; questioning with a desperate need to understand why this cruelty existed and where it came from originally.

Author's Note

The next chapters in this story are told by Eva, someone who, when faced with trials, had to find her inner strength with a determination never to give up hope and believing everything would work out. Eva remained in the belief that good actions overcome all trials in life because when tested you find out who you are by your will, your choices and the actions you take.

Chapter Two

WE RETURNED HOME and Pete made tea. I sat staring at the plate in front of me. I was aware of Pete's anger and shame at his own actions, but I was also aware I had to be very careful what I said and how I behaved.

'I think I have a bug, Pete; I'm feeling sick.' I said this so as not to upset him and to cover any emotion that may be shown and fuel his anger, whilst desperately trying to cover up my own grief over what had taken place. I carried on with the pretence. 'I feel sick, Pete.' I did indeed feel sick, a different kind of nausea, sick of it all.

Pete looked at me, then replied, 'Eva, go to bed.'

I quickly headed for my room. I was exhausted, and I didn't want to be there anymore, I couldn't stand it. I could see Pete was angry because he knew what was wrong with me but he couldn't mention it either, because he also knew why, a painful truth he did not want to be reminded of, so I went to bed.

*   *   *

'Morning, Pete.' I pretended nothing had happened. I could tell Pete was looking at me as if he were about to either explode or have a breakdown. I could not afford to escalate this situation. Pete placed a plate on the table; breakfast consisted of two slices of toast but I couldn't eat them.

Pete looked at me. 'Well, what are you waiting for?' he muttered without looking at me. 'Get them down you, you haven't got all day, you've only got ten more minutes.'

My eyes were swollen from endless silent crying and I could feel the emotion returning again. One teardrop hit the plate and I quickly wiped it away.

Pete was annoyed. 'Stop being so stupid, Eva, and eat your toast!'

I could feel the heat in my skin, the lump in my throat. 'I don't feel well, Pete, that's all it is.'

'Get to school, Eva, there's nothing the matter with you.'

I left the house, closing the door behind me. I cut through the park on the way to school.

Chapter Three

I HAD COOKERY first lesson. I didn't have the ingredients for the recipe again, so I'd have to use the same excuse as last time and every other time I hadn't had them. Mrs Caring, my cookery teacher, was an average-sized lady who wore glasses. Her hair was mid-brown and very short. She had a habit of raising her voice when addressing me whilst looking over her glasses; she often spoke about her pupils as if she had some kind of ownership of them and it was apparent you had to do things exactly the way she wanted, no questions asked. I knew she would be standing in front of the class as usual with her lack of compassion and lack of understanding of my situation. What was worse—facing Miss Caring, or facing Pete to ask for eggs, butter and flour?

I entered the classroom to hear my cookery teacher shout my name. 'Eva Rose!'

'Yes, Miss Caring?' I answered.

'Well, have you got your ingredients for today's class? Are you going to surprise us with your excellence of memory?'

Of course, she had to stand on parade in front of class when saying this as the whole class had to witness my ridicule. I wondered why she never sang my praises in the same manner. I wondered if it made her feel more important to do this, but I didn't really care. All I knew was others reacted to her ridicule and it was costly for the one being taunted and this added to my overall disappointment. Today wasn't a good day for me to just go along with it. As I glanced around the room, I could see some pupils remained quiet though in nervous disapproval, also aware they could be next if they stepped out of line. In a strange sort of self-preservation, I pretended to tolerate her.

'No, Miss, I forgot, Miss.'

'Just get out.' She pointed to the door.

On my way out of class I could hear a snigger, then a drawing of breath which was followed with 'Miss, she's really naughty, isn't she?' There was the sound of giggling coming from one of the girls in the class; it was Grace Young, who sat at the back in every lesson. I knew Miss Caring liked her as her voice was so much softer when she spoke to Grace, making her a good example of what Miss Caring expected as a code of conduct to be followed by all.

Grace was taller than me and taller than most of the girls in the class; her hair was shoulder length and she usually wore it up in a scrunchy way that always matched the colour of her uniform. Grace had the most perfect fringe, not a dark brown hair out of place. I listened to her remarks as I passed her leaving the classroom. She was enjoying every moment of my embarrassing exit. I'm not sure why but that girl gloated every time and took great pleasure in my failings.

*   *   *

School was out, and walking through the yard I was careful not to look at Grace who was standing with her friends. I hurried past holding on to my satchel and looked to the floor as I did so. I cut through the park on my way home.

I loved the park with its stunning array of colours, the many different flowers, the smells of honeysuckle and roses and the grand standing trees. Every time I passed through was an experience I savoured; its ever-changing patterns were always beautiful. There was always something new appearing or returning from the soil, the dirt; hills with hidden pathways, overlooking an old ruin which stood proudly against the backdrop and was part of the scenic magical view of the park; from a distance it looked like an ancient castle. I followed the paths knowing where each one led, each with its own perfect spot, one overlooking bright yellow and orange daffodils which grew down its banks, another overseeing green lushness and bluebells everywhere, like a blanket of calming, peaceful colour coating the ground. I loved the bluebells. In between them were small clusters of white bells and other paths led to roses, beautiful blooms of all colours. The light breeze blew their scent towards me and I raised my head to catch the full aroma. With my eyes closed I inhaled the exhilarating scent. There were lots of trees in the park of all varieties, beech trees, large oak trees, fir, chestnut and sycamore trees. Some were evergreen and held their leaves and colour in the winter; some lost them and stood in their nakedness until spring arrived again and they gave birth to new growth. It was summer and in the summer all the leaves were bright and showed their many shades of green. As I tried to take away the thoughts of sorrow, I focused on a positive thought. Tomorrow was another day, when there was drama with my favourite teacher, Mr Burley, who had dark mousey blond hair with a touch of grey to the sides; he had a bushy moustache and was a warm-hearted man with a friendly face.

Mr Burley had a very distinguished look about him. He usually wore a tweed jacket and a tie to match his trousers, sometimes a dicky bow and both usually a different colour to his jacket. Drama was a lesson I looked forward to and I think others did too.

Chapter Four

'**OKAY, HELLO, PEOPLE**,' Mr Burley shouted across the hall while rubbing his hands. 'Let's see what we have today.'

'Hello, Mr Burley.' It was always a pleasure to be in Mr Burley's class. He was sitting on the stage tapping his foot in the air. I sensed he was intuitive as he knew how to bring out the best in others; he made everyone feel like they belonged. I knew the other children felt the same way, for everything was just better in his class; he was always inspiring and encouraged us to do the same. He wasn't the run-of-the-mill kind of teacher and I thought he made a difference to how we learned. He had a unique way of teaching people with an understanding of those who attended the lesson.

After class Mr Burley pulled me to one side. 'I'm going to ask your guardian if you can go to a school of arts, that is if you would like to go. I think you have a talent.'

'You think so, Sir?' I replied. 'Really? Thank you, Sir.'

He followed it by saying, 'It's a boarding school which means, of course, you wouldn't be at home, you would be staying there; however, they will focus on your strengths. I believe it will be good for you but what's more important is what you believe, so give it some thought.'

'Sir, you mean that I would *live* there?' I asked. 'That's just great, I mean it sounds great, Sir, it really does.' Clasping my books in my hands for the next lesson I felt so light, as if I was walking on air. No one could move the smile from my face. It was so big my cheeks were aching. The feeling was like going to the beach; that moment when you see the sea and all you want to do is run towards it. I was so happy and I couldn't wait to tell Pete. Pete, yes Pete! Just for a moment Mr Burley had taken away the grief and despair. I thought to myself this was my chance to leave it all behind me.

*   *   *

Entering through the front door, I shouted, 'Pete! Pete!' I ran into the kitchen to tell him the news. 'I'm going to a school of arts. Mr Burley, my drama teacher, is coming to see you to sign the forms, so I can go. He's going to have a talk with you about it.'

Pete turned sharply towards me. 'Don't be so stupid, Eva, who do you think you are and who the bloody hell does Mr Burley think he is? Mr Moneybags no doubt—these things don't come cheap and he shouldn't be filling your head with nonsense! He better not show up here!'

Pete didn't make idle threats. What would I say to Mr Burley?

*   *   *

I couldn't mention it in class. Mr Burley found me in the corridor at school the next day. 'Hello, Eva,' he smiled.

Before he could say another word, I interrupted him. 'Sir, I have changed my mind. I don't want to go to that school.'

He looked at me, trying to seek a possible reason for this sudden change of heart. 'Why, Eva? It could be so good for you, and I think you would do really well there.'

'I just don't want to go, Sir. Sorry, Sir.'

'I'm sorry to hear that, Eva, but you have your reasons. However, if you change your mind let me know before the end of the month and I will see what I can do.'

'Thank you, Sir.' Walking down the hall I could feel the lump in my throat getting bigger. Fighting off the tears, I tried to put it out of my mind. That was the end of that. His kindness will always be remembered.

Chapter Five

A S I WAS WALKING through the park on my way home, I saw a girl from my school. She looked stuck on the bank. I had seen her before many times in the schoolyard after lessons. She always had brightly coloured ribbons in her hair, which was light blonde and styled in two high bunches. She sometimes wore coloured hair clips either side that matched her ribbons. She was a bit of a loner and usually stood looking at the flowers that grew in the window boxes around the schoolyard. I said hello and asked, 'Are you okay?'

She'd got caught trying to get up the bank but it was steep and there wasn't much of a path on that part. 'I think I'm okay,' she replied as she slipped back even further. It didn't seem to bother her much as she carried on with the conversation. 'The nettles got me on the leg.' Pointing to the area of her leg where she was stung, she explained, 'I'm trying to get that dock leaf.' She then pointed to a random cluster of large green leaves; they were known as dock leaves for their healing properties—known especially to relieve nettle stings.

I reached out. 'Here, take my hand. I will pull you up. What's your name?' I asked.

'Lily,' she replied.

'I'm Eva. I've seen you at school. Do you live in Blanch Street?'

'No, I live in Camelot Place.'

'Oh! It's nice there. I live close by in Pittington Street.'

Lily then took the dock leaf she managed to grab and rubbed it on her leg against the area she was stung. 'Thank you,' she replied, then threw the leaves over the side of the bank.

I explained how much I love the park and enjoyed going off the beaten track, following untrodden areas in the park. I then invited Lily to join me. 'Do you want to see where that path leads, Lily?' I pointed towards an opening in the shrubs.

'Oh yes,' she replied.

I showed her and we climbed through some hedges, then scrambled up the hill to a spot high up overlooking the park below.

'Oh wow!' Lily gasped. 'What a view.'

'You can see the whole park from this spot. I'm not sure if many people know it's here,' I informed her. We sat and looked over towards the flower banks, laughing at the hilarity of people passing who were oblivious to our presence being there as we listened to their conversations. Then I realised the time. 'I have to go now, Lily. Pete will have my tea ready. He's my guardian.'

'Okay,' Lily replied and just seemed to accept most of what I said, not questioning my personal views but quizzing me about some other things. She was funny and a little strange and I sensed wiser than she appeared. Walking back through the park, we were laughing and talking about school and the fact we were off the next day for the beginning of the six-week summer holiday.

'I'm going to the beach tomorrow. I can't wait.'

Lily asked, 'Can I come?'

'Yes,' I replied. I was happy she wanted to. I really liked this new friendship.

Lily then arranged the meet. 'Shall I meet you at the bridge next to the shop that sells all the old stuff, the one with the mummy case in the back? Do you know which one I mean? The shop owner always wears a flower in his hat. Do you know it?' Lily explained then added, 'I think he's a little mad, you know, but in a good way.'

I knew exactly what she meant. 'Yes, okay, meet you there. What time?' I asked.

She arranged the time. 'Is 12 o'clock okay?'

'Yes, that's great. See you tomorrow, Lily.'

'Bye, Eva. See you then.'

I felt I'd made a friend who was very unique but so was I. Grateful and pleased to have made the connection, I ran home.

Chapter Six

THE NEXT DAY I met up with Lily and we headed to the beach. When we got there, we sat on the cliffs overlooking the sea; calm, slow rippling waves made their way to meet the sand, then withdrew again into the sea back and forth with white foamed edges, separating each wave as a discrete part, then as each wave overlapped another returned back to part of the whole sea.

Lily removed her denim backpack and placed it on her knee, then removed a small neatly wrapped package and held it under my nose for a second. 'Banana sandwiches,' she smiled. 'My mum made them; do you want one?'

I thankfully accepted. Lily handed me a sandwich and I took the first bite. 'Delicious,' I said. The banana was mushy and sweet as it squeezed through the bread. Afterwards we made our way to the beach and walked along to the far end towards some caves.

Lily looked behind, then turned to me saying, 'What's going on there?'

I looked and could see some girls from my school. There were three of them and one was Grace Young from my cookery class. The three girls were walking a fair distance behind. I tried to put as much distance between me and them as possible so I began to pick up the pace. Two of them were getting closer and they noticed me. One shouted over, 'Look there's "eggcellent" Eva.' The rest started laughing as she repeated what Miss Caring said in class, 'Get out now!' followed with laughter and a condescending tone.

'Like you never heard that before,' Grace shouted over and the others joined in with the humour. 'Like every lesson,'

Grace again cruelly jested, following again with mocking laughter.

'I'm just ignoring them,' I said to Lily. 'They will get bored.'

As I walked on, one of the three called the other two back to look at something they'd seen on the rocks in the shallow water, the others rushing to see. 'See you later, Eggy,' shouted Grace as she clambered up the rocks.

I headed for the caves with Lily, relieved they were heading in the opposite direction. The caves were high, making it easy to walk into, and deep, stretching as far as thirty feet. On entry the noises faded; there was less chatter from the people on the beach.

'They say someone lived in these caves,' I informed Lily.

'Yes, I know,' replied Lily, who surprised me again as she knew all about it from a story her grandmother had told her and who sounded amazing from what I heard. Lily went into great detail about her grandmother as we walked. I suspected there was going to be many more of these stories to come. We went even further into the cave where there was a small entrance at the back, wide enough to manoeuvre ourselves into. Just then Lily asked, 'Why did that girl call you eggy, Eva?' Then added, 'You don't have to answer if you don't want to.'

I replied, 'I often forget to bring the ingredients for the recipes needed for cookery lessons, and I get told off for it and they find it hilarious.' Then I said, 'Actually, Lily, I don't forget but it's not important.'

We had been in the caves for a while and it was quiet, but the silence was broken when I heard shouting and my name being called. 'Eva, Eva, please come help me!' It was Grace Young. I could hear her in the distance. At first, I thought they had followed us and I was going to be in for more teasing or worse, as I knew where these things can lead to.

When I came out of the cave, I could see just one girl. I was right. It was Grace, but she was alone on the rocks; her

16

friends had left her and she was crying. For a slight moment I felt an urge to be happy at her expense; after all, she was always having a dig at me so why shouldn't I enjoy this moment? But for some reason I couldn't, and I couldn't leave her to cry. I noticed the tears in her eyes. She was on a large rock; she wasn't in danger as the water was shallow, but the water was surrounding her and it had clearly given her a fright. The other two were laughing and had run off. They could see I was going to help her, so I guess they left thinking she would be okay.

'I'm stuck,' she cried in a panic-stricken voice. 'The tide's coming in. Get me off here, please, Eva, get me off here.'

I could see from afar her friends shouting and laughing on the promenade as they made their way back up the banks heading away from the beach. I suspected they had some kind of falling out between them and as they could see I was helping Grace, they may have believed it safe to leave her. Well, I use the term *friends* loosely as clearly, they were not her friends as they certainly weren't very friendly.

Grace and I watched from the beach as her so-called friends were heading in the opposite direction away from the beach and then disappeared over the top of the cliffs as they went out of sight. I called to Grace, 'Jump!' but she was very afraid and by this time she was hysterical. I climbed up the rocks. The water wasn't deep but Grace was still panicking.

'It's okay. Look I'm standing in it and if you like you can climb on my back. I will pull you over.' I looked at her face. I was so used to seeing her differently at school. Here it was again, that polarity; power and powerlessness facing each other. *So strange*, I thought, *what is power and why does it exist?* I thought, *Is it a choice or is it an action?* In that moment, I was experiencing it from the opposite extreme. I didn't have much more time to dwell on that thought. I reached out my hand and shouted, 'Come on! It's going to be okay. Look at me!' as I drew her attention to where I stood in the water, which was by this time above my knees. I pulled her over into the water.

She was still afraid but I said, 'It's okay, I've got you, Grace,' and helped her onto the sand.

I could see she was really upset, but it's not just the fact she got stuck on the rock that upset her; her friends had run off—they had let her down. She also showed herself in a different way to me of all people. 'Are you okay?' I asked.

She looked at me, surprised. I could see it was bothering her as she half looked away. 'Yes, I'm fine,' she awkwardly replied, wiping away her tears with her sleeve. 'Thanks. I mean, like, for getting me off the rocks.' Then she smiled at me again. I hadn't seen that before either; I mean, I have seen her laughing and usually at me, but this time she was smiling with kindness.

'It's okay as long as you're okay. You did great by the way, Grace. It was a bit of a scramble but you did it!' I chuckled. 'Scramble, get it?'

We laughed; however, this time was different, we laughed together, we laughed with, not at. I introduced Lily. 'This is Lily, my friend.' I could see that Lily was happy to be called a friend and she smiled too, placing her hand in the hip pocket of her purple corduroy dungarees.

Lily leaned forward towards me with her opposite hand that she then placed on my shoulder. 'Hello, Grace. Want to come to the caves?' Lily asked.

Meanwhile, I was thinking to myself, *Am I really asking my mortal enemy to hang out with me? This day just got really weird.* I didn't even like her, but looking at her I could see something was different. I think we both were changing what we once felt or thought about each other, all happening in that moment. I could tell she really wanted to come.

'I would love to,' she stated, then she looked at the sand, pushing it with her foot but half looking at me also. She paused, waiting for my reply or maybe it was my approval. I could see it meant something to her.

The girl from the cookery class seemed a million miles away and in the past; we were in the present moment now, about to change the future. 'So do you want to come?' I asked.

'Okay, if you don't mind. I mean, if you really want me to,' she said. Again, I saw Grace looking for approval, or was it forgiveness?

'Yes, of course I do, please do!' I replied. We smiled at each other. I thought, *Isn't it funny that a smile has no native tongue yet it can be understood in every language when it's sincere.*

Lily had entered the cave by this time and I could hear her as we followed. 'Look at this!' Lily's voice bellowed. She had wandered off and found something right at the very back of the cave. It was another cave directly behind with a small opening. The tide by this time was right out and the sand had been pulled away showing an entrance to a third opening. We went inside. I had never seen this far into the caves before. On the side of the cave wall, we could see there was some writing but it was very confusing and wasn't making any sense at all. 'What do you think it means?' Lily asked.

'I'm not sure,' I replied.

'It's like a foreign language,' Grace answered.

The writing read as follows:

There's a bridge between land and sea allow that bridge to
(there were spaces, as the wording was so faded on the cave wall it was impossible to see what it all said, but between the faded spaces it went on to read)
from cave to heads, stones and beds form a fitting circle
(then said) *these words you read are in your hand*
to make a turn to see the plan.
Beginning, middle O the end, but make the same
or change and bend, or if you can, to make amends.
This will be seen by very few,
be brave, be strong, to clear the view.
From height and root, what passes by,
wind catches sail and then we fly.

19

It didn't make sense, well not then anyway.

Lily then piped up and said, 'What if a million years ago people lived here and spoke this strange language and they didn't have any paper so they put it on the cave wall?'

I said to Lily, 'Yes, and if you are going to speak a gibberish language you might as well put it on a cave wall.' We all laughed, made up silly words and gave them meanings. I said it could have been called 'Seaglish'. Grace replied, like a secret language that only the cave people understood 'Cavelish'. We looked and talked about our ideas as to what this text could possibly be. It became the topic of some excellent stories and adventures inside our heads.

We chuckled and Lily said, 'Well I'm not sure about you two but I'm having my "banawich".'

We all burst out laughing.

I said, 'You're having a *what*?'

Lily then replied, 'A banana sandwich, "banawhich".'

Before we knew it, we were making up more silly words in laughter whilst we shared the last two sandwiches between the three of us. We gave things nicknames and the beach became 'WR', short for water, pronounced as 'Wer' and the name stuck.

After the laughing stopped, Grace leaned towards me saying, 'Eva, I'm really sorry for calling you names in cookery.'

I could see how much Grace wanted me to know this. 'Forget it,' I said. 'Everything is different now. We're good.'

We headed back and we started walking along the promenade. Suddenly Grace's mother appeared and was shouting over towards us. 'Grace, is that you? Come on. I've been looking all over the place for you.'

Grace started to head towards her mother and as she waved goodbye I shouted up, 'We are meeting at twelve tomorrow if you want to come to the beach, that's if you're allowed?'

She shouted her reply with a smile. 'Yes, great, the WR.'

We all laughed as we arranged to meet again at the shop owned by the strange man with the flower in his hat. Lily and I shouted, 'Bye,' and waved again as we started walking home.

On the way back Lily looked at me, then nudged me. 'Chuffing heck,' she said, laughing. 'I didn't expect that, did you?' Meaning the whole change of events with Grace.

I laughed. 'I know. Earlier I thought she was going to punch my lights out.' We laughed again. This was the beginning of a wonderful friendship. Who ever knew these friendships would share amazing adventures and that those adventures would create wonderful happenings in such magical ways?

Chapter Seven

THE NEXT DAY I skipped down the stairs. 'Morning, Pete.' I grabbed a piece of toast from the plate, put it in my mouth whilst putting on my coat, which was half on and half off, and headed for the door. 'I'm going out, Pete. Is that okay?'

Pete was a little quiet and I wasn't sure if it was because he was just relieved I was going out, or relieved I wasn't so upset. I guess it made him feel a little better. Pete then replied, 'Okay, not too late though.'

Hanging on to my coat with one arm through the sleeve, I ran out of the door looking forward to meeting with my new friends.

This time after the beach we hung around an old ruin overlooking a small dene and on the other side overlooking the park. The dene had an old horse and carriage track which runs through it and an old stone bridge. On the bridge was a small walled area made of large stones, just like the bridge, and it made a very nice seat to rest on. It sort of had a mysterious look to it, maybe because it was a little wild with its huge dangling roots winding and wrapping themselves around the sides below the bridge and its foliage cascading down almost reaching the ground. Maybe it because it was untouched due to very few people passing through, either way you could see nature doing what it knows best when left to do so. Sort of like some of the pathways in the park hardly trodden. I'm not really sure what it was I liked about it, but there was something mysterious about it, and I, Grace and Lily, agreed there was something very special about the place indeed.

Walking through the dene we went to explore the nearby graveyard and as we did so we noticed one of the graves had a headstone showing the same markings as that which were on the cave wall. Similar to the cave wall was the wording, which looked like some kind of poem. It was a large headstone, a strange, eerie looking one which stood out from the rest. It wasn't like the others as it was covered in moss, grass and weeds that were overgrown. We moved the foliage aside and pulled away the weeds to reveal the wording. On it was a poem we could read easily but like the cave wall writing, we had no understanding of what it meant. There were also markings, and some sort of picture, numbers too; it made no sense, but as we saw it, there was a connection to the writing on the cave wall because they were identical in style. There was a definite similarity between the texts. The poem on the headstone read:

> *Life's tapestry and heartfelt eye,*
> *big change comes from butterfly.*
> *Past and future a present brings*
> *a change as subtle as it moves its wings.*

This made no sense to any of us whatsoever. Lily made a joke about how our own made-up words had more clarity. There was a picture of what looked like clasped hands and a circle shape. Lily said, 'That's weird, my grandmother used to say something like that, something about we are all a tapestry of past, present and future.' Now all of these things were starting to take effect as we curiously pondered in silence for a moment.

Grace was thinking out loud. 'Hmm, hmmm, I'm not sure what to make of it,' she said, as she stood rubbing her head, messing up her perfect fringe. We decided we needed more research and, on our way home, we made plans to return the following day.

*   *   *

23

The following day Grace, Lily and I met again. We just stuck together after that, sometimes meeting at the beach, the park, the graveyard or the dene. We became very close to each other and found excellent places for the imagination to while away the hours, thinking about being adventurous. We discussed many things about the mysterious cave writing and what it possibly was and the writing on the headstone, but we never shared our thoughts with anyone else. We agreed we must find out what it all meant to understand the connections. We decided to get a pen and some paper and write down the text when we got back to Lily's house. Lily handed me a notebook and pen, so I became the keeper of it.

* * *

The next day we went to the cave at 6am. It was early but the tide had to be fully out to be able to enter. When we got inside the cave, I made notes. The pictures on the cave wall showed what looked like a piece of cloth that had some kind of trimming or edging; there was a jewelled ring, a spiral of some kind that we couldn't quite make out, but I drew it as we saw it and hoped for the best. Between the words were numbers that looked slightly different from those of our present time.

Well, that's what I made them out to be. I still couldn't help but notice the connection and the similarities between the two pieces of text. We then went to the graveyard and looked at the engravings on the headstone.

A tapestry was mentioned in the poem on the headstone, and I supposed a tapestry was material; we were only guessing, of course, but on closer inspection the cloth did look like a tapestry on the cave wall, but it was difficult to say, maybe a connection, we thought. The numbers were identical on both the headstone and the cave wall, and this started our intuition. We were just guessing and, to be honest, at the time we didn't really know what we were doing. We were just enjoying the excitement of it all as we made our notes.

Chapter Eight

LILY had a computer in her bedroom and her mother allowed us to do some research; as it was history she didn't mind us being there—she may have been thinking it was for school. To be honest, we didn't say it wasn't. Lily's mother was always very glad to see me and Grace and the feeling was mutual. I believe she liked to see us inspiring each other and, I suspect, to see Lily making friends as she was a bit of a loner. Lily was like her mother and, by the sound of the stories, her grandmother too. They were all called Lily after the first namesake which was Lily's great grandmother. Whilst on the computer we studied language and different text styles to gain more understanding of what it all meant. Searching any connection to the texts, we found some wording to be of an ancient language. It matched the notes we had taken so we compared the texts.

Placing both texts together, we began to notice that they were not only similar in style but both were some sort of poem or riddle. The more we looked at them it seemed they could even possibly be some sort of a map. We were very excited at whatever it was, that's for sure.

Gravestone writing:

> *Life's tapestry and heartfelt eye,*
> *big change comes from a butterfly*
> *Past and future a present brings*
> *a change as subtle as it moves its wings.*

Cave writing:

There's a bridge between land and sea
allow that bridge to
(between the faded spaces it went on to read)
from cave to heads, stones and beds
form a fitting circle (then it said)
these words you read are in your hand
to make a turn to see the plan.

Beginning, middle O the end,
but make the same or change and bend,
or if you can, to make amends.
This will be seen by very few,
be brave, be strong, to clear the view.
From height and root, what passes by,
wind catches sail and then we fly.

After taking notes we left Lily's house and hung around the graveyard, then as usual we gravitated to where there's a small church and there we sat, inside the doorway for a while talking about what we wanted to be when we grew up.

Grace said, 'I know what I want to be, I want to be a huge corporate businesswoman in charge of lots of people with such a large house and to be really powerful and have lots of money.'

I said, 'Do you really, Grace? Why is that?'

She looked at me and said, 'Well, doesn't everyone?'

'I don't know, do they?' I spoke. 'It sounds very grand; what would you do with all that power and money?'

'Well, lots of things,' Grace went on to say. 'I would help parents not have to work so hard and spend more time having fun. I would have the best of everything, everyone would like me.'

I laughed and said, 'Grace, I like you just the way you are.'

Grace then looked at me and Lily, saying, 'I'm so glad we are friends.'

We spoke about how happy we were to know each other and how knowing each other made a difference in the way we thought about ourselves and how we were able to be ourselves, almost like we were meant to meet. Grace asked me what it was I wanted to be. I replied, 'I'm not really sure, I will have to think about it.'

Lily said, 'I think I know what I want to be,' as she smiled looking at a daisy.

I asked, 'What's that, Lily?'

'A gardener. I would very much like to be a gardener. I want everyone to see something beautiful growing and I want to be part of that. It would just make me really happy to think I created a smile in the eye of the beholder.' Lily smiled whilst standing with one hand on her chest, then went on to say, 'A beautiful picture made with flowers, an experience that brings joy.'

This was so Lily; a beautiful daydreamer and why I was so glad she was my friend.

I thought about how we met in the park and what the park meant to me and others, how it was important to have someone looking after these places because they are for everyone and meant something to those who attended. I could see Lily as a gardener.

Lily then jumped up and down with an excited look on her face shouting, 'That poem! That's it, high and rooted.'

We had no idea what she meant. Then she pointed to the huge tree and said, 'It's high and it's low and it's rooted.'

We approached the tree. There was a picture of a ship and sails on a stone that was beneath it and what looked like a number was suddenly clearer and it looked like an arrow of sorts. It matched the engravings on the gravestone. The arrow on the stone pointed towards a picture of an old door. I recognised it. I thought, *Where have I seen this door?* Racking my brain, it came to me. It was the door of the ruin! I knew it definitely was as I knew the building well. I shared this with Lily and Grace, and this drummed up more excitement; we three still had no idea what we were doing but it was fun, so we carried on. It was also starting to get late so we decided to head back home but made plans to return the next day.

Chapter Nine

G RACE, Lily and I ran to the ruin the next day. I looked around the doorway scanning the area for clues. At the bottom of the wall there were gaps in the floor and it showed depth or space below it. It was difficult to see, but there was some kind of drop under the floor deep underground, and we circled the area to find anything that could be a possible entrance. From squinting through the cracks in the floor we could see there was a drop leading beneath the fireplace looking like it could possibly run further.

The fireplace had a huge chimney, a little broken down at the top but still intact at the base. It was a large fireplace, large enough that you could stand under it. We couldn't see anything else of note at that time, nothing else that could be linked to the writing. It was a little frustrating but still exciting; we really hoped it was going to lead us to something and we kept the momentum of hope. Even though nothing was discovered we kept our interest alive.

Lily said, 'Isn't this fun?'

I replied, 'It certainly is,' and we carried on.

* * *

After a while Grace and Lily started messing about slightly, giving up on the hunt to find more clues. Grace stood under the chimney and started to make daft noises that made an echo and which suddenly gave me an idea. I decided to see if sound would travel; maybe it might give some clue how far the possible passages underneath went. By listening to how my voice travelled from one side to the other it might show there was an actual real basement to the ruin and not just ground giving way. Lily ran to the first crack in the floor and crouched down towards it, then shouted through it and I placed my ear to the ground at the opposite side. I listened as Lily shouted down through the space between the cracks at the base of the wall and the floor. Lily shouted, 'Helloooooo!' I could hear her plain as day. There was definitely an underpass or tunnel of some kind running under the opposite end of the building.

Grace still had her head in the chimney by this time, making silly but funny noises of her own. We ran towards her as she was only half listening to what we were doing. Grace was having fun but we managed to convince her that this needed more investigation and we all agreed.

We decided to rest for a moment. Messing about on the old ruin was too much fun and we sort of left the trail there just for a little while and danced around the building exploring everything. I went inside the chimney and was laughing at Grace who was holding a stick she had picked up, holding it like a staff in her hand whilst thrusting the stick towards the ground. Next to the ruin, in a deep, comical voice, she began to shout, 'Old ye building reveal your secrets!' We were all laughing at this point, and I lost my footing and stumbled. As I did so, in an attempt to regain my balance, I grabbed a brick that was protruding on the inside of the chimney to stop myself from falling. It moved, and as it did, I could hear a noise of motion. I crouched from under the chimney and looked towards Grace and Lily who were looking back at me.

The girls shouted, 'Eva, are you okay?' They too knew at once something wasn't right just by looking at my face, we were so in tune with each other and could read each other well.

I said, 'Did you hear that?'

'No,' said Grace.

I beckoned Lily to come closer. Lily approached me so I asked, 'Lily, can you lift me up so I can reach?' I wanted to investigate from which direction the mechanical noise was coming from. I moved my hands around the inside of the chimney, feeling around the area where the brick stuck out. Above was a gap that wasn't there before I stumbled earlier. I began to feel all the space around the brick. I placed my hand inside. There it was, I could feel something, it felt hard, it felt rectangular in shape. It was a box. I was a little scared but excited, surprised and curious and all at the same time.

Chapter Ten

WE PLACED THE BOX down on the ground behind the ruin and sat down on the grass so we were comfortable when we opened it. We prepared to see what was inside. The box was rectangular with four small legs that curled outwards. Inlaid within it, it had what looked like shell; it was all very natural-looking and the triangular shape above with four sides were leading to a point at the top.

Grace eagerly said, 'Open it!'

Lily watched me as I slowly started to open the box. Inside was a ring, just a plain band, nothing fancy but it looked very old. The ring was made of wood. You could see the grain on the inner side. There was silence for a moment as we all looked at it, all excited to find it, not knowing why it was there or how special it was or who it belonged to. It was just a small box and a small plain ring.

I slowly placed the ring on my finger. This was when everything changed! All I could see in my field of vision before me was a blur, as though my surroundings were whizzing by. The images flickered past me before my eyes very quickly. Time was moving but I wasn't sure which way, and I suddenly began to panic. I quickly took off the ring and was back in the present moment.

Lily looked at me with a startled expression on her face. 'What happened there?'

'Why?' I replied, wanting to know what happened to the present moment as my time was moving in many different directions.

'You were gone for a second, Eva.' I looked at Grace who looked astonished. 'Eva, you just disappeared!' she said.

I knew then this was not a plain ring; in fact, there was nothing plain about it. Was it some kind of transportation device? Maybe, I wasn't sure. I tried using logic in my own mind. I may not have known where it took me but I knew I returned safely when I removed it from my finger. I used that to measure the risks of putting the ring back on my finger, not really sure about anything else but my curiosity grew and got the better of me and I wanted to see more. Intuitively I had a feeling I would be alright.

I offered the others a try and Lily said, 'What if we hold hands? Do you think it will take us all?'

'As long as we are connected it should do,' I said.

'Let's do this together!' Grace exclaimed and I agreed.

I asked Grace the time as she was wearing a watch. She looked and stated it was 2.22pm. I looked at Grace, then at Lily. 'Okay let's do this, but we need to check the time afterwards too.' It became apparent to me that each clue we stumbled upon led through our intuition to this very moment and that nothing was accidental.

We held hands tightly and Lily placed the ring on my finger with one of her free hands, thus forming a sort of crescent half circle. Just then the images in front of us changed and we felt like we were being thrown, like something was thrusting us forwards while we were still tightly holding each other's hands.

Suddenly the motion began to slow right down until we came to a stop. As we stopped by accident we broke hands, but we still remained, thankfully, in the same place together. Later, I deducted from this that forming a ring of hands gave the connection we needed to allow movement together back and forth in time; this is what allowed us to travel or move together through time. We were able to remove the ring when we arrived at the destination. Holding hands again would allow our return as long as we were all connected to each other and the ring.

We looked around to gain clarity on our surroundings. We had arrived in front of a building. It was a very tall building, as big as a hotel but I didn't think it was a hotel because there were no names though there was a doorway. We entered. Inside the building were many rooms and we could hear voices and music and people, so we followed the sounds. I had a feeling it was the right place to go. The noise was a party! Everyone there was wearing suits and pretty dresses and there were bottles of champagne on the tables along with fancy food and cakes, beautifully decorated and lined up on ornate cake stands. There were chocolate fountains with pieces of fruit on stands lined up in a very organised fashion. There were flowers on the tables next to tall silver candelabras. The candles were lit and the flames flickered causing a subtle light to spread from their burning wicks. I could see the flickering of flames that distributed the light onto the golden table covers.

Everyone in the room was congratulating a woman who was standing on a stage which was situated at the back of the room facing the party of people. A woman was holding a mike and the party seemed to be for her. 'Well done!' one man stated whilst shaking the lady's hand as she was returning the thanks, but there was something about her reply that felt sad. She was smiling but her mood wasn't flowing with ease and her eyes were speaking so loudly that it overshadowed the smile. We looked at each other and saw that we had all noticed this too. I was thinking to myself, *Why so sad? Yet everyone is cheering her.* A man raised his glass in the gesture of a toast saying, 'Here's to a woman who can rule with her head.' She gave thanks but it was clear to me this was not an authentic expression of gratitude. Maybe I was reading too much into this, but it was as if she didn't mean it. Something was missing. Maybe she felt undeserving of the thanks or she was unhappy with what she was being thanked for. If anything, she looked slightly displeased.

I stopped overthinking it when she held the mike to her mouth and said, 'Guys, enjoy the food. It's late and it has been a long day. I have an early morning ahead of me so I'm going to leave. Thank you, all.'

Maybe she was tired, I thought to myself. We decided we had seen enough and we again held hands spinning off in a different direction. It didn't take as long this time to stop. When we arrived, we were back in the same place; it was the same building but this time we were inside the building in a different area, a corridor in front of a different room. Instead of people cheering we heard something else.

This time we could hear someone crying. Curiously we opened the door. Inside was a huge office that had thick wooden panelling all around the walls. There was a giant heavy wooden desk and the same woman who was on the stage at the party was seated at it holding a telephone. She was on the phone talking and crying to someone, saying that she wasn't happy about some kind of sale. I could hear her say she didn't want to go ahead. 'Home House is important,' I heard her say. 'I'm not sure we should. It's the only home for some of the children living there.' She went on to say, 'Sure I'm a businesswoman and yes, I can rule with my head but I have a heart too. I know it's a lot of money but not everything is about money.' The woman put the telephone down and sat looking at some drawings of which there were many, sheets and sheets of them, sketches, plans, each one showing a grand building and land and other prints showing redevelopment ideas of some sort. She was so upset she still hadn't noticed us standing there. She didn't notice until Lily said, 'Hello, Mrs.'

The woman jumped from her seat, startled at our presence. 'Oh my word!' she exclaimed. 'How on earth did you get in here?'

Lily answered, 'We have a magic ring.' Grace nudged her trying to hush her up about the ring.

Luckily for us, the lady wasn't angry at us and she smiled; her eyes were smiling this time, too. Lily's comment made her go from tears to laughter. 'I have no idea how you got through security but I should get someone to take you kids home. Let me contact your parents.'

Lily, dismissing what the lady said, looked at the many papers on the desk, approached her and asked in a very matter-of-fact way that only Lily could: 'What's that? What are they for?'

The lady looked and smiled at Lily and replied, 'I'm not actually sure what I'm doing with them at this moment.'

With that Lily looked her straight in the eye and said, 'You could house a lot of people with that huge house. I bet there's lots of wonderful things you can do with that.' Lily then went on to say, 'You could do some good with that, I bet.' Lily had a way with words and was always tending to good ideas. 'What about a lovely park around it? You could teach people to garden.' Then she went on about how she loved flowers and what flowers she could plant. 'I bet it's got a huge kitchen. You could feed a few with that too.'

I laughed as I could see the lady's smile grow even wider. Joining in on the momentum, Grace and I laughed. Lily looked very seriously at us for a moment; then her smile broke out across her face and we all joined in the laughter.

Grace looked at the woman and said, 'I do think that's a very good idea. I'm sure you will do something wonderful with it, whatever you do.'

The woman intensely looked back at Grace. The two locked eyes for a few seconds. The woman smiled, then shook Grace's hand, wanting to, I feel, humour our grand ideas in a very adult fashion. She went on to say, 'That sounds like a very good idea indeed.'

Grace looked surprised and replied, 'I feel it's rude to call you Mrs. May I ask what your name is?'

The lady was just about to say something, but was interrupted again by Lily who had been panicking about being away too long and then said, 'I think it's time to go home now.

We have been here some time and I don't want my mother worrying about me.'

I moved closer to Grace and held her hand and she took Lily's holding it tight. Replacing the ring on my finger we three hoped and prayed it was going to return us safely to where we originally found the box. Thankfully we returned safely and we were very pleased we did. We all sat on the grass back where we originally started.

Grace said, 'It would have been nice if the lady finished what she was going to say. I would have liked to know her name.'

The time was 2.23pm. Only one minute had passed but so much had taken place.

We questioned where to hide the ring and I said, 'I believe this ring has been hidden for a long time; the gravestone and the ruin are so old, I think it will be safe placing it back in the box.' So we returned it to where we found it. We made a pact to not speak to anyone of what we had seen or where we had been. We kept the pact.

Chapter Eleven

T HAT WEEKEND I was worried about placing the ring on my finger. I wasn't sure why or what I was afraid of, it just hung around me like a shadow. What might I see next? What was ahead? Questions unanswered. What was going on with all the strange happenings? I mentioned it to Grace and Lily and we all had the same concerns, but we all felt intuitively compelled to continue.

We got to the ruin the next day and removed the box from the chimney. We looked at each other, holding the ring, and took a step forward closer towards each other again in a sort of half circle, ready to clasp hands, and Grace placed the ring on my finger. This time we arrived in a different setting. It was a bright, sunny day; the feeling of a warm breeze touched my cheek as we stood in the middle of a field. I knew this field; it was close to the banks of River Stone. Memories of the past came flooding back from the day the pups were thrown into the river and I had to prevent my tears welling up. I thought of something else and moved to a feeling of calm, looking at the flowers in the long grass. I then heard the barking of a dog in the distance. Just then, out of the blue, a huge dog came bounding over. It crashed into me and knocked me from my feet; its tail wagging, it covered my face with its tongue. It was such a friendly dog and it appeared very happy to see me, bouncing up and down, licking my face. I stroked its fur and with both hands rubbed its ears. I rolled on the grass giggling as it pounced this way and that over me in a playful manner.

A woman came running over the field, following after the dog, shouting, 'It's okay, he doesn't bite.' When she got closer to me, she called to the dog, 'Here, boy; here, boy. I'm so sorry,' she said, 'he's so friendly he just loves everyone. Here, let me help you up.' She reached out with her hands which were as soft as her smile.

I jumped up and exclaimed, 'Oh, it's okay, no harm done. He's lovely, I don't mind.' The dog stood wagging its tail whilst I stroked its soft fur. 'It's a lovely dog. I'm not afraid in the slightest.' I asked the lady, 'What's his name?'

She replied, 'His name is River Stone but we call him River for short.'

I was still for a moment, again knowing fine well what River Stone meant to me. The unhappy memories of what happened to the puppies came flooding back. River Stone was the name of the river that carried the sack, and it was a reminder of my helplessness to stop what happened on that dark day. I was curious to know why this lady chose that name for her dog as much as I was curious as to why we arrived in the very same place.

I asked, 'Why did you call him River Stone?'

She went on to say, 'Five years ago my mother and I were walking along River Stone bank, and my mother heard the sound of a young girl crying. It was so loud and sorrowful we ran to see what and who it was as we were in fear she was in danger. When we got there, there was no sign of her but lo and behold there was a sack in the river! We could hear whimpering coming from inside the sack. My mother and I leaned over from the side of the riverbank and with a stick managed to hold on to the edge of the sack and drag it from the water. Inside the sack were puppies! Three to be exact. We took them home; they have been family ever since.'

I looked at her as tears fell down my face. The lady looked at me and softened her voice and said, 'Hey, it's okay, they were all saved. This one was the first out the bag so we named him River Stone, after the riverbank.'

I wiped my eyes with my hand then shook her hand with both of mine almost forgetting to let go. 'You are a very lovely lady. A very, very lovely lady indeed,' I said.

She laughed and then thanked me, then rummaged in the large cloth bag she was carrying over her shoulder. She then handed me some peaches. 'Here, for you and your friends.' As she handed them to me, she said, 'I own a fruit shop in the next village. I can spare these, there's plenty more where they came from. Enjoy your walk, girls.'

We all thanked her. I cuddled River Stone one last time as he licked my face, then the lady and the dog named River, one of my very own puppies who I now knew was safe and well, left. As they almost faded out of sight River turned and barked as if to say goodbye, but I felt it wasn't goodbye. For some reason I had a feeling we would meet again and he would be as glad to see me again as we all were today.

We three held hands again; looking at each other I had a feeling that Grace and Lily knew we had seen everything for today that we were meant to see.

Chapter Twelve

IT WAS ANOTHER DAY and we were back at the ruin. We took the ring from the space behind the brick. By this time we were more understanding of what we were doing.

Grace looked at me and said, 'Ready?'

I replied, 'Ready.' I turned towards Lily. 'Ready?' I said and Lily nodded as we drew closer to clasp hands and we spun off again, arriving this time in a huge gardened area. This garden was somewhere unknown to the three of us, yet it was also familiar. We looked down at a lady knelt in a garden area; we couldn't see her face as it was hidden under a large-brimmed floppy hat. She was wearing brown trousers and a floral shirt with lace frills. We had arrived slap bang in front of her as she was kneeling down in a flower bed.

'Oh, my word, girls, you startled me! You can't just creep up on an old lady like that.' Thankfully the lady was amused as much as she was startled. After all, we had just appeared out of nowhere. She had a kind smile and a very kind, I would say almost perky, face. 'Well run ahead girls,' she said, laughing. 'There's free cake and juice up at the house. I presume that's what you are here for?'

We had no idea what she was talking about or what else was happening but we liked the idea of cake and juice. We ran through the garden and along beautiful winding pathways with neatly floral borders in the direction she pointed to see what was going on. I couldn't help but feel the familiarity once again but I could not quite put my finger on it. At the top of the garden was a grand building, a huge stately home which I also had the feeling I had seen somewhere before. There were people outside and the sound of instruments coming from inside. There was a large thick wooden double door which had a huge brass handle in the centre. We opened the door and entered.

Inside the building were children; some older and some with parents attending what looked like some kind of a summer fete. There was an array of arts and crafts. Some of the children displayed their paintings and others displayed different kinds of art such as pottery pieces, pretty serving plates and jewellery. In another part of the building, we could hear singing and in another an orchestra played. Lily stopped to look at a painting. It was a painting of a tree in a field of flowers under a sunrise. Lily looked on at it for a little while. The others playing music in one room were packing up their instruments, and there was a rushing of people carrying bits and pieces to and fro, one carrying a trumpet, another passing by practising singing and the sounds of *me me me me, la la la la* amongst other similar noises echoing around. A ballet dancer with her hair elegantly drawn in a bun danced by us, dressed in a light pink leotard and a white tutu. She kicked her leg forward as she glided by whilst making her way to another room. It was very busy but a truly wonderful sight with so much going on.

Just then a voice came from behind saying, 'Would you like some?' When we turned to see who it was, a boy was standing there holding a tray of delicious cakes with very fancy icing, paper plates and lace paper doilies. We each took a paper plate and placed a cake upon it. The sweetness of the icing melted into the cake as I took the first bite. It was deliciously mouth-watering. A lady who was holding another tray kindly offered us a glass of juice which we polity accepted.

'Thank you,' I said to the boy handing me a slice of cake.

'That's very kind of you,' Lily said.

The boy smiled back at Lily and replied, 'You're very welcome.'

There was a ribbon stretched across from one end of the patio in front of the house to the other and everyone gave a cheer when it was cut. Lily asked the boy, 'What is that?'

He replied, 'It's the grand reopening of the home. We are all glad to get back to normal as we have been sharing rooms whilst the work has been carried out.' The boy pointed towards a winter garden and an extension of some sort. He then said, 'That's what the celebration is for; there has been a refurbishment.'

Lily asked the boy, 'What is this place?'

The boy replied, 'It's Home House. It's where people like me learn different skills.'

Lily questioned the boy further. 'What kind of skills?'

The boy replied, 'Skills like singing and art. I play in a band. This is where I learned to sing and play an instrument.'

Lily looked at the boy and said, 'I would like to hear you sing. I bet you have a very lovely voice.'

He replied, 'I would sing my best song if you were listening.'

I looked at Grace as she nearly sniggered at the awkwardness of our being in the presence of Lily and the boy as they blatantly flirted with each other through their compliments. We managed to keep it together long enough for them not to notice.

He smiled at Lily again and said, 'I watched you looking at the painting of the tree.'

She replied, 'Yes, it was my favourite.'

He said, 'Mine too.'

I could see by this time Grace was gearing up for another snigger, so I pulled her towards me saying, 'Grace, did you have some juice?' Then I told Lily, 'We will come back shortly.' Lily smiled knowing I was really giving her time to get acquainted.

I pulled Grace into another room which was empty. I could see through the crack in the door; there was a painting above a mantle of a lady sitting at a desk. 'I think it's her,' I whispered to Grace, then louder, 'It *is* her, look!' It was the lady who was crying, the same lady who was at the party.

'Yes,' Grace said, 'and I think this is the same building from the sketches she had on her desk.'

I knew I had recognised the building. 'Don't you see, Grace, she didn't sell the building after all; she made it this home for children and families to learn.' I ran back for Lily. 'Lily! Lily! Look at this.' I grabbed her hand and took her into the room. Lily came, following as she wanted to know what all the commotion was about. 'Don't you see, Lily, you told her to do this.'

'Did I?' Lily looked confused as she questioned what it was she had done.

Grace said, 'Yes, Lily!'

We began dancing at the fact that something so amazing had taken place and the fact that we helped create it all because of a kind, thoughtful idea which came from Lily. What a day, what a beautiful day indeed! The puppies, the home, the wonderful people we had met, everything was beautifully perfect. Lily couldn't believe that the lady actually took her advice.

I turned to Lily and said, 'Lily, never underestimate the power of a good intention, a sound mind and a good heart.' I'm not sure where that sentiment came from but I believe it's true.

It was a long day and looking much brighter than when we started out; in fact, it was becoming pretty amazing. Walking back from the house through the park, we reached the lady in the large floppy hat who was still digging in the garden. Lily ran towards her and asked about the lady in the picture on the mantle. 'Who is the lady in the painting in the chair?'

The lady in the floppy hat turned towards Lily in reply, 'Well, that lady's name is Grace.'

I looked at Grace and smiled. I had a feeling about something but wasn't really sure just yet if the feeling I had was true.

Lily said, 'Thank you, Mrs, it's been a really wonderful day and the cake was delicious. I love your flowers by the way.'

The lady looked up from her floppy hat once again, placing her small garden fork in the ground whilst wiping the soil from her hands to reply to Lily. 'Those are called lilies, my dear. I'm glad you like them as they are my namesake. My mother named me Lily and there's a few generations of us Lilys,' she said, laughing.

Lily in joyous reply said, 'Me too, and my mother's name is Lily too, how very odd indeed!'

We were just about to say goodbye when the boy whom Lily had been talking to came running after us asking if we were going to be returning sometime soon. We knew very well he really meant Lily. We said, 'We hope so.'

Lily asked his name and he replied, 'Hugh.' He noticed Grace looking at me smiling. We really tried not to giggle but it was beginning to show. The boy went bright red in embarrassment and then ran off, but not before turning to Lily to say, 'I'm looking forward to seeing you again, Lily, when you return.'

Lily also blushed, replying, 'Thank you. Goodbye, Hugh. Hope to see you again.'

We prepared to leave, looking for a place to hold hands to return back home. When we got back Grace and I were so excited from the day's events, we were talking over each other. However, Lily was silent, which wasn't really like Lily at all; then it dawned on me that though Lily had such a brief encounter with Hugh, it had a considerable impact on her heart. I approached her saying, 'Lily, I truly believe you will see Hue again. I just think sometimes things have a way of working out.'

It cheered Lily up greatly and, of course, I had no idea if it was true, but I hoped it would be for Lily's sake.

Chapter Thirteen

BACK AT HOME I noticed Pete was busy doing work on the house. I really wanted to say the puppies were fine but knew I had to keep it to myself. He was doing his work and for the first time I could see him differently; he was tired, working so hard. He worked day and night and still couldn't make ends meet. I could see it bothered him greatly. I wondered, did he really ask for this life and if so, what was there to learn from it? I asked him if he wanted a cup of tea.

He looked at me. 'That would be nice. Be careful with that kettle,' he shouted into the kitchen as I was filling it with water.

'I will be careful,' I replied. He expressed care; it wasn't often shown but it was there in places, I guess.

*   *   *

The next morning, I got ready for school. All I was thinking of was going back to the old ruin for the ring and for another adventure with my friends.

Again, I got into trouble for daydreaming in English and I knew cookery was going to be another ordeal. I braced myself for another show of Miss Caring's delightful quips of the day. When I got into cookery class, I could see Miss Caring looking at me ready to ask if I had the recipe but before she could say a word Grace shouted over, 'Eva, you forgot something,' then she handed me a bag. Inside the bag were two eggs, flour, butter and a small bag of sugar.

I whispered, 'Thank you,' and I made a cake in cookery class; it was the very first time I had the ingredients for the recipe and it came with kindness, not the kind of flamboyant 'look how nice I am giving someone something' kindness but the silent, unspoken kind that doesn't need to be advertised.

It came from a friend who was once an enemy; it was a sure thing that we can learn to like someone with understanding, compassion and kindness. You see, Grace never really knew me and I never really knew Grace because we weren't really being ourselves at all. I took the cake home and told Pete it was a free recipe day at school. It wasn't a lie as it was a recipe given to me freely.

I got a knife and placed the cake on a plate and put it on the coffee table for Pete to slice. I went into the kitchen to make a cup of tea for Pete and whilst doing so I could hear him shouting with joy into the kitchen: 'This is the best ever, it's fantastic!'

I laughed aloud saying, 'The cake's not that good. It's a bit dipped in the middle.'

He said, 'No, not the cake, but it's a very nice cake, it's baked perfectly.' He then went on to say, 'I got the job I went for.'

'That's fantastic news, Pete!' I shouted back from the kitchen. 'Hooray! That's brilliant news.'

Pete explained, 'There's a lady who owns a fruit shop in the next village—she has accepted my application and she wants me to run the shop. The owner is taking part in another business venture and she wants me to manage the shop to keep it open. It's a lot more money than I have ever earned, so it means fewer working hours too.'

I said, 'That's wonderful, Pete.'

Pete continued to finish the conversation, saying, 'It's a full-time position. It means I can leave the factory and the warehouse.'

This was marvellous news. I was so happy for Pete. I gave him a hug and said, 'Pete, I think everything is going to be alright.' Then we sat and ate the cake with our cup of tea to celebrate.

Pete then looked down. I watched the smile slowly leave Pete's face as he looked at me. He was almost in tears and his voice was breaking. He said, 'I am so sorry about the puppies.' He tried to explain that he also ran back in a desperate act to find them but they were gone. I don't think he really meant it to happen; something had taken over him and I could see the regret. He wasn't a bad person. I think people do better when they know better, and I think he was beginning to change— there were a few differences. People make mistakes, I guess and I wasn't going to judge him. I was feeling far too happy for that. As often as I looked at his angry face, today I had seen a victim of circumstance and whose actions were changing and whose circumstances were changing too. *He* was changing—it wasn't just the job; there was something else working inside him. I wasn't sure what but whatever it was I was grateful.

Chapter Fourteen

WE WERE RESEARCHING the history of the ruin during the week after school on the internet at Lily's house. Lily's mother was always cooking something lovely for us and we usually had biscuits afterwards. The wording from the cave and the gravestone we couldn't put a date to but the ruin was dated to 1877. It appeared that when the ruin was built it had an additional use which was to look after people in the village; it was known as the safe house where those in need came to stay. The people who lived there were three couples. One of the ladies bore a striking resemblance to the lady in the photo, and Lily mentioned how another was familiar to her having a striking look of her grandmother. I kept going back to the poem about the tapestry; past, present and how there was a connection to the people we met, the names being also Lily and Grace. A strange coincidence? The pups we knew were connected to my own past. With all these connections we got to thinking and came to the same conclusion which placed us all in a state of bewilderment.

'Lily, do, you think that the lady who was in the garden wearing the floppy hat could be one of your ancestors?'

Lily replied, 'Yes, I do and I don't believe these adventures are accidental either, the places and people we meet or where we land.'

Grace added her theory to the conversation. 'Then do you think there's a possibility that lady whose name is Grace has something to do with me?'

I knew Grace had worked this out also. I then made another deduction. 'Do you think it could be possible that the lady in the garden who was wearing the floppy hat could also be you, Lily, not an older relative?' I explained my outcome. 'You see, going from the clothing styles which are not of any historical fashion style that I know of but not too dissimilar from today's, her mention of her ancestors fits yours too, Lily.' I was guessing by the clothing and the ages too, in fact, most of what I was saying was based on a hunch. All I knew was that everything was connected. I did conclude that each time we had used the ring so far was a timeline that had some kind of change for the better. It was all still pretty much a mystery to us why any of this was happing or why it linked to us, but I understood there were no accidents here.

Another connection I made was a conversation I had with both Lily and Grace about what they wanted to be when they grew up, and that Lily was the gardener and Grace was possibly the corporate boss in these timelines just like they wanted to be in the now. I fathomed that we had maybe changed some decisions which affected our future selves. Maybe the part of the future I was meant to see was the puppies being safe. I contemplated what could happen during our next travels.

Chapter Fifteen

I T WAS SATURDAY afternoon and we made our way to the ruin. We took out the ring as usual from the space inside the chimney and replaced the box, then we sat on the grass. As we did so, we held hands and prepared to venture to another timeline. This time, we arrived in a changing room; we walked outside entering into a clothing shop. There were many extravagant designs on the shop rails. Ladies' fashion was on one side, with dazzling dresses, gentlemen's garments on the other. The first thing that caught my eye were the hats; some with feathers, some with bows, some resting on mannequin heads, and others sat on display above large colourful hat boxes. Ladies were there trying on hats whilst looking in mirrors, some trying on dresses, making their grand exit from the changing room.

On the opposite side of the shop were men's suits, some of which reminded me of my drama teacher's tweed jackets. There was a finely dressed man trying on a waistcoat and cloth cap. Like the ladies' fashion there were top hats, flat caps, fedoras and trilby hats and more of all shapes and sizes. I watched on as a man stood in the walkway in front of another mirror, looked down towards another man who measured his outside leg with a tape measure holding various pieces of material over his arm whilst doing so.

We made our way out of the shop to gain some idea of where we were. Opposite the shop there was a small open hut full of reading material where a man was selling newspapers. He was shouting. 'COME GET YOUR MORNING PAPER. FRONTLINE NEWS, ANCIENT PIECE MISSING FROM MUSEUM, YOU HEARD IT HERE FIRST!' Held up in his hand was a newspaper with a picture, a photo of what I presumed was the said ancient piece and what looked like a piece of clay pottery, possibly a vase which also sported the same markings as those from back home on the cave wall. We knew we had to go inside the museum so we asked the man for directions. It was a very short walk away.

The museum was enormous. It had large glass doors and two security men stood trying to organise the crowds of people that were coming and going. Past the doors and through the entrance were about fifty people. We squeezed through, past the hordes of people, making our way to the main floor. The museum was so busy inside, with more security, and there were news reporters everywhere trying to take photos as the staff tried to push them out the doors. We made our way through each floor and looked around the museum. There were so many things to see. On one floor there were relics of different origins and lots were adorned in gold; a statue of a woman wearing an ornate headdress, bangles, and jewels that glittered under the lights as they were neatly positioned in their glass cases. We moved up to another floor; there was a huge dinosaur, fossils of sea life, impressions of their skeletons imbedded in rock, and stuffed animals. A ferocious lion, a tiger and monkeys. All were set in a background that matched the settings of their natural habitat. On the next floor, I stopped to look at a statue of a lady dressed in Victorian clothing who was standing at a piano. The dress she was wearing was the colour grey and around the edges was layered lace-filled petticoats. A bustle was at the back and the front of the dress was drawn up at each side revealing an underskirt of a slightly lighter colour. We looked further and there were old-fashioned dolls which also represented the ladies of fashion; their faces were made of what looked like porcelain and their eyes appeared to follow us around the room as we passed by.

The dolls were also wearing pretty hats and bonnets tied with silk bows around the neck with hair all neatly presented in curls.

On the same floor was a classroom with wooden chairs and wooden school desks and ink wells. The desks faced a blackboard with chalked etchings across it on the wall, and there was a wax figure of a teacher facing the front of the class holding a narrow stick which pointed towards the blackboard.

Entering the lift, we moved to another floor where we visioned classic cars and models of cars with leather interiors, some with headlights that protruded out of the front of the vehicle. I imagined they illuminated the road ahead when in motion. Further on were real train carriages. We were allowed to be seated inside. A man who was dressed up in a very old-fashioned ticket collector's uniform gave us a ticket as we imagined the destination. When he said we had arrived, we jumped out and waved with thanks. There were fire engines and more wax figures of men putting out a fire with a hose. There were wax figures of soldiers too and pictures of soldiers, some in red uniforms, others in green. I spotted a letter next to an old tin cup. The ink was clear and it was to his family and it said *I can't wait to get back home, lots of love, Alfie.*

On the next floor were Egyptian figures, some coloured in shades of vibrant blues and gold. In the corner of the room, stood against the wall, was a case standing over five-feet tall. It was closed but painted on it was a man wearing a headdress and next to it was a mummy inside a glass case. I recognised this from school and there was one inside the antique shop back home. There were vases of all colours, headdresses in glass cases and jewelled broaches and tiaras. There were statues of all nature of men and women in various poses. With cameras flashing constantly the light was so bright it was obstructing some of our view. There was so much to see and it was so busy our eyes diverted from each other for a few minutes and as this happened Lily suddenly became caught up in the crowd. I tried to get to her but it was impossible to reach her.

I shouted over into the many people towards Lily as loud as I could: 'Don't worry, Lily, we will find you, just don't leave the building!'

Lily was very upset and I was worried, so was Grace who was hanging on to me so we didn't lose each other. We tried to scramble towards a space in the room that we could ask for help and Lily was by this time out of sight.

Just then I heard the voice of a lady call towards me with a huge camera around her neck. She was holding Lily's hand. 'I think you're looking for this one, girls,' she smiled.

Grace and I looked around to see the lady and a police officer and Lily who was with them both. We were so relieved to see Lily. Grace, Lily and I thanked the lady who explained that she was a reporter and that she had managed to pull her from the crowd. The police officer told us to be careful and we made our way towards the exit. Lily went on to say that because she was so upset the lady had to keep wiping her tears with a hanky. I hugged Lily. We thought there had been enough drama for one day and that we should head back.

We arrived back at the ruin and returned the ring behind the brick in the chimney, then sat on the wall next to the ruin overlooking the dene.

We were ready to go home when Lily noticed she still had the handkerchief that belonged to the lady reporter. When she unfolded the handkerchief, she noticed there was an inscription. It said *To my dear friend Eva, with love, Lily*.

I was aware then that the timelines we all entered were becoming personal. Could it have even been myself in another timeline that found Lily in the museum? And this woman who had given lily the handkerchief: was she a stranger? Who was she?

Then for us to visit this place in a separate moment in time—it was all very confusing. Still we had no idea what these connections meant between us or where they were leading or what the significance was of the events that took place, but the words of the poems kept repeating in my mind:

Life's tapestry and heartfelt eye,
big changes come from butterfly.
Past and future present brings,
a change as subtle as it moves its wings.
There's a bridge between the land and sea
allow that bridge to (between the spaces I read on)
from cave to heads, stones and beds
form a fitting circle these words you read
are in your hand to make a turn to see the plan.
Beginning, middle O the end,
but make the same or change and bend,
or if you can, to make amends.
This will be seen by very few,
be brave, be strong, to clear the view.
From height and root, what passes by,
wind catches sail and then we fly.

Chapter Sixteen

THE FOLLOWING DAY at Lily's house we made notes of all the things that connected us, all the events that took place. The building, the house, the names of the people. We were all so grateful to be part of this adventure, but we were also wanting to understand how and why it was all taking place. We spoke about how we were also friends connected by different circumstances; how we helped each other against all of the odds. Grace and I from enemies to friends and Lily, who needed encouragement to believe in herself!

Grace talked about her circumstances at the beach and how it changed her and we believed we were guided in some way, to what exactly we weren't sure of but we were aware we all needed each other. We went on to each adventure after this day with courage, knowing whatever came up was for us. We believed our actions made a difference; even the smallest kind act helped others in such an enormous way it appeared to have a ripple effect. Then the poem again came to mind that even a butterfly's wings can change the course of the tide in another part of the world. This was encouraging. We went forward to each future adventure looking and listening closer to find the hidden meanings so we could contribute whenever the situation revealed itself and look for the connection of all who were part of this story. We believed we were changing the future by the actions we made. We wondered if there had been anyone before us who may have found the ring in another timeline. Lily said her grandmother often used to say, 'There are no accidents, no mistakes.' I couldn't agree more.

*   *   *

The next day we went to the ruin with a 'ready for anything' kind of attitude. We went forward together, landing this time in the past. A young boy was sitting on some steps which led to the front door of his house. The boy was crying and he was a little dishevelled in looks with torn clothing. We saw what we believed to be his parent open the door and pull him up the stairs. Why he was in tears waiting to be in the house we weren't sure. We could see there was little love there as kindness was surely missing from the sharp actions.

We went to the window and looked through. Inside the house he was playing with a toy soldier, then sat at a table to eat. After that he was given food, and shortly after he was pushed out of the door back on the steps again. We asked his name and he replied, 'Pete.' I went to him and he smiled. We asked him what was around the area as we tried to make more sense of the surroundings. We comforted the boy who was around our age and said, 'Pete, do you want to know a secret?'

He replied, 'Yes please.'

I told him, 'It's going to be okay, just have faith in that everything is always working out for you.' I told him to keep an eye open for magical things, then told him the only reason we must have been here was to pass that message to him. He smiled and I asked him to remember me because it was important to do so. I searched for something to give him to hold on to, something that he could remember us by.

Lily had a few bits in her pocket and one was part of a broken hair slide. It was a small plastic yellow circle. She said, 'Here. Keep this to think of us.' He said he would. Lily said, 'I have another and I'm going to keep it too.'

He smiled and thanked us. We wanted him not to lose hope so we decided to leave in front of him, we knew it would reinforce what we told him. Lily took out the other hair slide that matched the one she gave him as a keepsake before we left and she waved at him with it.

We were so happy to see the look of surprise on his face and a huge smile followed by laughter as we left. We continued visiting the ruin where strange and wonderful things were happening and in each and every event when we arrived back home changes were ongoing in the present also. Pete's new job was taking effect on him in a positive way and he was happy with his new change of circumstances. Everything was working out for the better. He was now working full time in his new job and fully managing the fruit shop. He said he hadn't met the owner yet but they were constantly speaking through email. All was well.

*   *   *

As the year passed, our school days came to an end. We were older and a little wiser and ready to leave the school. Just as Lily dreamt she would, she chose horticulture as her profession following her passion, and Grace in her turn went into business following her wishes also. I took up a new job in a small town not too far away as an apprentice reporter covering small local stories. It was okay, I was happy and I made a living from it. I was seeking true stories of this and that and writing about them. I carried on in this role for a while with an eye for adventure. I paid special attention to each experience I came across because I, of course, knew there was a reason for every season in every chapter of life.

Lily excelled in her skills and was responsible for amazing gardens, some of which would appear in magazines and she continued to grow with a passion for flowers. Every time there was a before and after photo it would be a colourful masterpiece just like she always wanted. Every garden Lily worked on was filled with love and showed splendid arrangements of colour that she created with her beautiful presence. Grace became a huge success too. She was very ethical in her approach to her work. She was moving in very important circles and adding to society in very positive ways.

I was moving with the flow of what was happening day-to-day and treating everything like an adventure. We were arranging meet ups in between our working life to again join hands and take the ring on another adventure but there wasn't many more to come.

On this one occasion, we arrived back at the house and this time we arrived inside. Through the window we could see across the beautiful gardens. There was another celebration of some kind, this time slightly different as the tables were in rows inside and outside of the building. A man and a woman were placing food on one of the tables outside, so we went to investigate. Lily was so pleased to be there as she never forgot the young boy and this was her chance to tell him how she felt. After all this time she still remembered him, but when she queried about him the replies were blank—it was as if he had never been there which was very strange. She explained everything in great detail about him and it troubled her that he wasn't there and that no one could recall him. I tried my best to reassure Lily by saying who knows what's to come in the future. She smiled but slightly reluctantly. It was difficult for her but she positively looked up and said, 'Eva, this must be a chapter of a story unwritten, I'm sure.' And this time she smiled with faith behind her words.

The man and the woman who were placing food on the table added a warmth and a humorous feeling to the celebration. As the man reached forward across the table of food, he picked up a small pie and started to eat it. The lady had just placed it on the table shortly before. She gently tapped his hand and laughed, slowly shaking her head with a smile, and I heard her say to the man, 'Pete, what are you like?' in a fond way. She then looked at him and laughed. From the way they behaved I could see they were clearly a couple. I recognised the man called Pete; I knew him—of course it was my Pete and I could see he was very different from the old Pete.

There were children there and one of the girls was chasing after a butterfly and caught it. 'Let it fly,' the man named Pete said. The girl smiled and let it go.

The woman shouted over: 'Pete, my love, come get this plate and put it over there.' She pointed to the end of the table and went on to say, 'Place it in the middle so the balance is right.'

I heard the name again and understood this was indeed Pete my guardian. I looked a little closer at his clothing and could see he was wearing a very odd tiepin; it was a plastic yellow circle, the kind you get on a child's hair slide. I think you know the type I mean. How things had changed so very much. He was so happy and who was she? Pete went from one extreme to another. Here he was saving butterflies. I was so pleased about this but he was also very different in my present too—there was some kind of magical shift. Choices and actions are very important. How we view things are too, I guess, for we always have the option to see things differently—a different perspective, who knows. Maybe life is a mixture of choices and outcomes.

We ate food there and our presence was never questioned at the house for some strange reason with its beautiful gardens which were all part of the experience that we were all part of. From where I was standing finally everything was coming together. The house appeared to be running well and people were still learning skills. There were just a few things I wasn't entirely sure about. Who was the lady running it., and who was the lady in the garden? Was there still something that had not become clear in this timeline? I still wasn't entirely sure where I fitted in. It wasn't so important, because everything was just how it should be. I was just glad to be part of it.

Chapter Seventeen

I OFTEN REFERRED to the riddle or rhyme. Maybe our lives are partly woven into each other's. From visiting the past and the future there was always a message for the present. All were affected by each other; a kind of cause and effect. When we create the cause, it in turn creates the effect. What we learned from each other was expanding the outcomes and the great thing about it was all who took part were connected for the better, creating the stage for more amazing future events to take place. I later found out that the lady who was with Pete was the lady from the fruit shop. He met her at work after a long point of contact via emails. Pete got to hear about the puppies and I guess forgiveness changed something in him. This is how I drew my conclusions: what was ahead was a mystery waiting to happen.

This day like any other day we arranged to meet and arrived at the ruin; we entered the same as any other day but when we looked for the box which contained the ring it wasn't there. The exit remained closed and we couldn't find any way to release it. After endlessly walking around the grounds, we eventually gave up while it was still light. We went from that to the cave just to see if it too had changed. When we got there the tide was out and it was still visible. We looked at the cave wall and saw that the markings were also gone. Whatever opened up in this timeline had closed the same way. We searched for the meanings in the rest of the poem but there was nothing to add or deduct. Our search came to an end as time passed, and we accepted and trusted that it was how it was supposed to be.

One day Lily rang and asked me to go and watch a band with her. Lily loved music and this was her favourite band. I went with her because I felt she needed the company of a friend. The band was playing quite a distance from where we lived which meant we had to stay in a hotel in another town. We managed to get booked up and made the journey through to where the band was playing. The band's name was Hue/Mans and they sang a song called 'Lily Love' which Lily actually loved and sang repeatedly as it was her favourite song. The song was soppy, but sweet. We had a front row view which meant we could see the band close up. We listened to the many songs and at the end of the show the singer looked down towards the audience and gave his thanks for their applause, then looking in the direction of Lily he stopped talking and looked at her intensely. Lily was equally as mesmerised at the singer in a returned gaze; their eyes held in a stare until he spoke to us and made a request for us not to leave the building after the show.

Lily was wide-eyed by this time and we were both excited. After all, he was famous and this was something to tell the grandchildren. At the end of the show the security team approached us and escorted us towards the door to the exit. As we stood outside no one came, but little did we know the singer was searching everywhere inside for Lily. We waited such a long time but there was no sign of him. Poor Lily, it seemed another let-down. I couldn't help remembering the lost boy from the house who she never got the opportunity to see again. I know she never forgot him and I don't think she ever met anyone after that. We waved down a taxi and we jumped inside. As the taxi was pulling out into the road there was a banging on the window. I couldn't believe my eyes—it was the singer! He asked, 'Where can I find you?' Lily shouted the name of the hotel he could reach her at and he said he would call that day. As we headed back to the hotel, Lily was so excited and so was I. We were in a state of joy at the unexpected turn of events.

Back at the hotel we sat and waited and when the singer arrived, he was carrying a painting under his arm. The singer handed Lily the painting and explained he had once found a ring in a box and when he placed it on his finger, it took him to a house which he visited regularly where he learned to sing and play the guitar, and that time had never changed when he returned. The house taught different skills to different people and one day a girl came to visit; her name was Lily and she loved the painting so much he asked if he could purchase it from the artist and brought it back with him, keeping it as a memory. The ring disappeared and he was never able to return. They discussed the encounter and the painting hung in their house many years after their marriage.

Lily and Grace met up and discussed their plans for the stately home that Grace had just purchased. They named it Home House. It was run by Grace and the gardens would be Lily's side of things. Thanks to our travels they knew exactly what they were going to do with it.

Chapter Eighteen

PETE MET THE OWNER of the fruit shop who was the lady at the fete who strangely enough was working on a project which, of course, was the house. After a meeting with Grace and Lily the plans took shape. The lady was called Agatha, and Pete was given some wonderful news and was so relieved that the pups were well. He was greatly relieved as he went on to start his new life. Pete took what he learned and applied all he had learnt to his new life. He and Agatha married and both became cooks at the house.

Lily's husband became a music teacher. I think the reason why we could not gain access to the ring was because there was nowhere else to travel to, as we were now creating the future from the present and the ring's work was done. There was a magic that surrounded Home House and its beautiful gardens. Had our journey come to an end? I couldn't say this was the end—perhaps merely the end of another chapter. There were more adventures yet to come and more secrets to unravel as my part was not exactly finished just yet.

I carried on doing my work as a reporter which took me far afield in different directions and I reported some very interesting stories.

Connecting the dots, I could see circumstances in life when we feel powerless against the tide. We can hold on to the thought that everything we do counts, with small actions and positive thoughts. So, it's important that we never give up on ourselves and others—we always have an impact on our surroundings. The powerful and the powerless are actually equally dependent on each other and change comes with understanding, and with understanding we can free each other by allowing a bridge for both to appreciate a grander design.

Whatever we believe, maybe we can hold on to a benevolent power that moves through the centre of each human being. If we find this, we can create amazing things.

The decision is important to be kind or good, to hold out a hand despite what we see around us to do otherwise.

A kind human soul can achieve many things and when they find other kind souls the outcome is always wonderful. We had a magic ring but most of all we believed and supported each other. A home filled with love and kindness is always going to create amazing experiences for all and Home House was filled with love and kindness indeed. Each classroom had a name; my favourite was the Burley Room. It held drama lessons, with its beautiful stage at the back and curtains of shimmering gold. It was named after a great teacher—this was my touch, for he taught drama at my school; but much more, he taught kindness and the importance of working together. Above the stage was a huge chandelier which when lit filled the room and its hanging crystals shone against the walls. I had the feeling each teacher was selected for their unique abilities; each taught in ways of excellence of the human mind, heart and spirit. The students were of a kind nature and good character; maybe they weren't always so, but somehow their spirit, like sails, set flight so that they might become their very best selves. If there's a polarity in our makeup, then for sure we can add to one side or another; maybe by seeing enough of one side we can have the perspicuity to choose another. A simple act of kindness can create and when we choose to be understanding of the space we share, we can bring hope to any situation.

Maybe we are part of each other's greater plan, setting the scene somewhere ahead. It's by understanding ourselves that we help each other. Maybe it also governs the way.

My role, I hoped, one day would change from reporter to a writer of stories from my many travels and adventures. I would like to travel around the globe as I am sure I have many more stories to tell.

I hope we meet on our next adventure.

About the Author

This is Mary Duffy's debut novel. A mother and sister, she likes to find a quiet spot between her working days to scribble creatively! She enjoys the countryside, coffee shops, friends and adventure. She believes that acts of kindness however small can make positive changes—a belief reflected in her writing. She likes to add joy wherever possible to most aspects of life. A deep introspective thinker, she says she can 'get a little lost' in her head which she uses as material when writing. She likes to leave the reader with something to think about that may also give the reader a few supportive thoughts of positivity. As she puts it: 'If you read this book and come away with a smile, I have fulfilled my goal.'

Printed in Great Britain
by Amazon

41475361R00046